Hank and Oogie

by Nicki Weiss

A Snuggle & Read Story Book

AN AVON CAMELOT BOOK

AVON BOOKS
A division of
The Hearst Corporation
1790 Broadway
New York, New York 10019

Copyright © 1982 by Monica J. Weiss
Published by arrangement with Greenwillow Books
Library of Congress Catalog Card Number: 81-7136
ISBN: 0-380-69872-2

The Greenwillow Books edition contains the following
Library of Congress Cataloging in Publication Data:

Weiss, Nicki.
Hank and Oogie.
Summary: When Hank goes to kindergarten, he finally weans
himself away from his dependency on his stuffed
hippopotamus, Oogie.
[1. Toys—Fiction] I. Title.
PZ7.W448145Han [E] 81-7136

First Camelot Printing, April 1985

CAMELOT TRADEMARK REG. U.S. PAT. OFF. AND IN OTHER
COUNTRIES, MARCA REGISTRADA, HECHO EN U.S.A.

Printed in the U.S.A.

BAN 10 9 8 7 6 5 4 3 2 1

HANK AND
OOGIE

for SUSAN and AVA

When Hank was one, Uncle Felix gave him a stuffed hippopotamus.

"Oogie!" said Hank, and from that day on the toy hippo was called Oogie.

Oogie sat with Hank in the high chair, watched from the windowsill as Mama gave him a bath, and slept in the crib with him each night.

When Hank was two, Aunt Minnie gave him a teddy bear. She put it in the high chair next to Oogie. But Hank plucked the teddy bear out of the seat, and threw it on the table, right into a big bowl of mashed potatoes.

"Hank and Oogie," said Hank, and he went on eating his banana.

When Hank was three, Papa picked up Oogie
and examined his ripped ear and missing eye.
"Oogie looks terrible, son," he said. "Wouldn't you
rather play with your truck?"
Hank grabbed Oogie out of Papa's hand.
"Oogie is beautiful," he said, and he walked out
of the room.

When Hank was four, Mama took him by the
hand and said, "You can leave Oogie at home."
It was the first day of nursery school.
"Oogie is too little to be left all alone," Hank said,
so Oogie went to nursery school, too.

When Hank was five, he and Mama and Oogie
walked to kindergarten. But when they reached
the classroom door, two boys came over. One
was carrying a football and pointed at Oogie.
"You play with stuffed animals?" he said.
The other was wearing a baseball cap and said,
"Big kids don't play with dolls."

Hank said nothing, and when Mama kissed him goodbye, he didn't try to take Oogie from her.

"You'll learn to get along without him," Mama said, and Hank watched them walk down the hall together.

That morning in kindergarten, they drank apple
juice and ate cookies. They drew with crayons
and painted with their fingers. They unrolled their
mats and took a short nap.
And Hank missed Oogie.

When he got home at lunchtime, Hank put Oogie in the chair next to him at the table. "I know it's hard for you to be alone," he said, "but school is for big kids. Big kids don't play with stuffed animals. You'll learn to get along without me." So Oogie never went to school again.

But as soon as Hank came home, he put Oogie in the chair next to him at lunchtime.

And when Hank took a bath, Oogie still watched from the windowsill.

And when Hank went to sleep each night,
Oogie was tucked under his arm.
"Isn't he getting a little too old to be dragging
that hippo around?" Papa said.

And then, one evening before dinner, Mama was doing the laundry. She held up one of Papa's shirts and shook her head as she looked at a big brown stain on the front of it. "My, my," she said, "this certainly needs a good washing."

Hank held up Oogie and took a long look at the stains all over him. "My, my," he said as he shook his head, "so do you." And he threw Oogie into the washing machine with the rest of the laundry.

Hank stood and watched as Oogie was twirled round and round. When the machine stopped, Mama took out the laundry and a very wet Oogie, and hung them on the line. "Come on, Hank, it's time for dinner," she said.

"But what about Oogie?" Hank said. "I never eat dinner without Oogie."

"It will take quite a while for him to dry, dear," Mama said.

Hank slowly followed Mama into the kitchen.
He sat down at the table and stared at the
empty chair beside him.

He looked at his bowl of spaghetti and meatballs.
"But I can't eat without Oogie," said Hank.
"I think you'll find a way," Mama said.

And he did.

His stomach rumbled. The spaghetti and meatballs smelled good. Hank picked up his fork and ate his dinner.

After dinner Hank went into the laundry room, but Oogie was still wet. Mama said, "Let's go upstairs and get you bathed."

"I never take a bath without Oogie," Hank said.

He went upstairs, took off his clothes, and looked at the bare windowsill. "But I can't take a bath without Oogie," he said.

"I think you'll find a way," Mama said.

And he did.
Mama put bubble bath in the water, the tub filled
with bubbles, and Hank stepped into it.

When he was in his pajamas and had brushed his teeth, Hank said, "I want to see if Oogie is dry yet."
But Oogie was still wet, and Hank said, "I never go to bed without Oogie."

He went up to his room, got into the empty bed, and felt the big space he had all to himself.

"But I can't sleep without Oogie," Hank said, and got
out of bed. He walked to the chair next to the
night table and sat down. "I will wait till Oogie is
dry," he said.

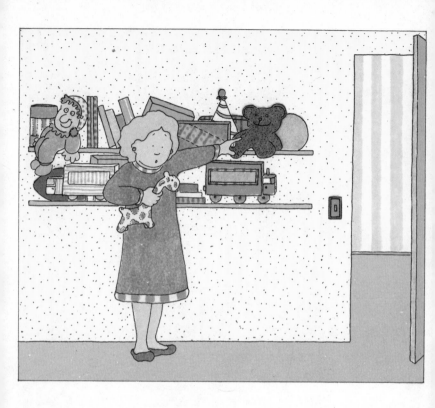

"Oh, Hank," Mama said, "it will take all night.
Couldn't Teddy help you fall asleep?"
"No," said Hank. "Too scratchy."
"How about Mr. Giraffe?" Mama asked.
"No," said Hank. "He smells funny."
"Well, I'm sure you'll find a way to fall asleep
without Oogie," Mama said, and she kissed him
good night, and walked out the door.

When she came back ten minutes later,
Hank was asleep in the chair. Mama picked him
up and put him under the covers.

The next morning Hank went down to the kitchen to eat breakfast.

"Hank, dear," Mama said, "Oogie is dry now. I have some more laundry to do, so why don't you take him and put him where you want?"

Hank walked into the laundry room, took Oogie and walked to the table.

But when he reached his chair, he paused for a minute, then went past it.

He went up the stairs, went by the bathroom where the sun was shining on the windowsill,

and walked into his bedroom.

He looked at the bed, at the chair next to the night table, then at the shelf of toys across the room.

"Yes, you are all dry, Oogie," Hank said, and he dragged the chair under the shelf. He stood on his tiptoes and put Oogie next to a big truck.

Now Hank is six. When he sits at the table, he talks about dinosaurs.

When he takes a bath, his tugboat takes one good shot at the tanker before the tanker sinks it.

And when he goes to bed each night, he takes
a book with him and looks at the pictures
before Mama turns out the light.

And the last thing he sees before he shuts his
eyes is Oogie, sitting on the shelf across the
room.